. . . for parents and teachers

To some degree all children experience the feelings that George does in *Sometimes I Don't Like School*. That numbing feeling of having to do something we're quite sure we won't do well is a universal sensation.

In this story George is encouraged to take a chance, stop his useless avoidance tactics, and, with support, face what appears to be an insurmountable problem.

While not totally mastering the situation (which would be unrealistic), George does solve his problem in a way that makes him feel proud and valued. His experience can thus be a springboard for discussion of any child's efforts at successful problem-resolution.

DAVID L. SMITH, Ph.D.
COUNSELING PSYCHOLOGY
MILWAUKEE, WISCONSIN

Copyright © 1980, Raintree Publishers Inc.

All rights reserved. No part of this book may be
reproduced or utilized in any form or by any means,
electronic or mechanical, including photocopying,
recording, or by any information storage and retrieval
system, without permission in writing from the Publisher.
Inquiries should be addressed to Raintree Childrens Books,
205 West Highland Avenue, Milwaukee, Wisconsin 53203.

Library of Congress Number: 79-24055

2 3 4 5 6 7 8 9 0 84 83 82 81

Printed in the United States of America.

Library of Congress Cataloging in Publication Data

Hogan, Paula Z
  Sometimes I don't like school.

  SUMMARY: After using various tactics to
avoid his dreaded arithmetic class, George finally
decides to face the situation head-on.
  [1. Problem solving — Fiction. 2. School
stories] I. Ford, Pam. II. Title.
PZ7.H68313Sq   [Fic]   79-24055
ISBN 0-8172-1357-0 lib. bdg.

SOMETIMES I DON'T LIKE SCHOOL

by Paula Z. Hogan

illustrated by Pam Ford

introduction by David L. Smith, Ph.D.

RAINTREE CHILDRENS BOOKS
Milwaukee • Toronto • Melbourne • London

Binnng! went the alarm clock.

George buried his head under his pillow, trying to block out the sound.

"It's Monday already," he groaned to himself. "I have to go to school. We're going to play that arithmetic game again. I'm no good at it, and all the kids laugh at me. Oh, if only I were sick, then I could stay home."

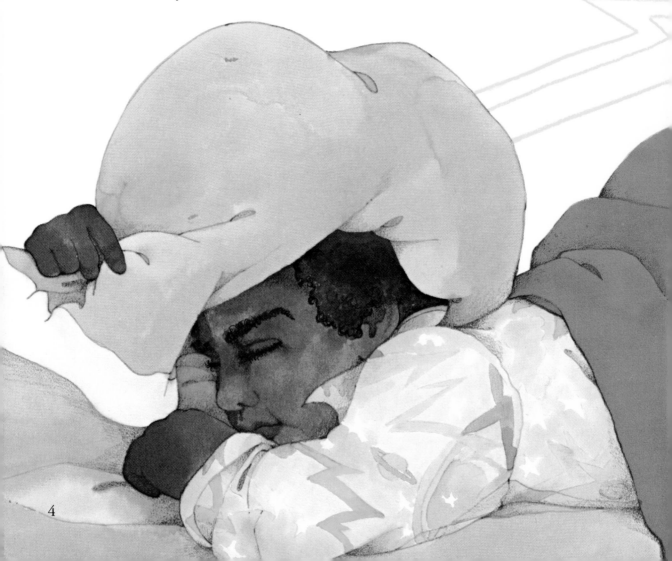

"Come on, George," called his mother. "I'm not going to bring your breakfast in there, you know!"

"I'm . . . I'm sick," George called back. "I have, um, a sore throat."

His mother came into his room. "Open your mouth and let me look." She felt his forehead. "You don't seem sick."

"Well, it's really my stomach that hurts. . . ."

"Come on, get dressed and eat something. If you still feel sick I'll call the doctor."

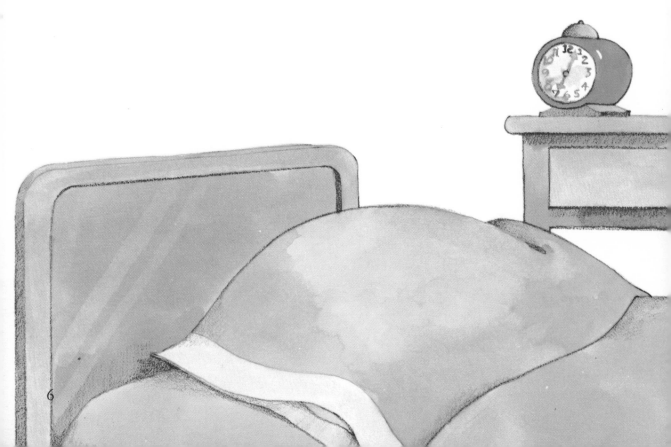

After breakfast George picked up his books.

"Thought you were sick," said his father.

"Oh, I feel better."

George knew he might be able to fool his parents, but he could never fool the doctor. He was too miserable to tell his parents the real reason he didn't want to go to school.

Every morning his teacher made the class stand up. Then she held up cards with addition problems on them. Everyone took turns giving the answers. If someone gave the wrong answer, that person had to sit down.

George always had to sit down after his first try.

As George walked into the school building, he had an idea. *I'll find a way to stop class,* he thought. *Then we won't play that dumb game.*

Inside the classroom, everyone was hanging up their coats and talking. George looked around the room and spotted the hamster cage in the corner.

When no one was looking, he walked over to the cage and lifted the door. A moment later, all four hamsters were crawling around the room.

George's classmates howled with laughter as they scrambled to catch the hamsters.

George's teacher, Ms. Green, wasn't nearly as happy. "Who let those hamsters out?" she demanded. She looked at a girl standing near the cage. "Maria, was it you?"

Maria was too shy to say a word. She just hung her head.

"I'll talk to you about this after school today, Maria," said Ms. Green. "All right, class, are all the hamsters back in their cage? Good. Let's get ready for arithmetic now."

George felt awful. Maria was taking the blame for something *he* had done. And he hadn't done a thing to stop the arithmetic game.

One by one his classmates took their turns at the game. When it was George's turn, Ms. Green held up a card that read "4 + 2."

George could feel his heart beating. "Uh, I know it . . . but I just can't think of the answer," he said finally.

"Take a guess," said Ms. Green.

"Five?"

The sound of giggling told George he was wrong. He slouched down in his seat.

Maria stood behind him. She almost always knew the answer. "It's six," she said softly.

"That's right," said Ms. Green.

I don't like this game! thought George. *And sometimes I don't like school, either!*

The next morning, George walked
toward school as slowly as he possibly
could. *If I don't show up,* he thought, *maybe
everyone will think I died.*

Then he passed by the field where he
and his friends played ball, and he had a
better idea.

It had rained during the night. Now the
field was nothing but a big mudhole.
George looked at the mud, and he looked
at his shoes.

He dropped his books on the sidewalk
and took a running jump.

Whoosshh! Down he fell in the gooey
brown mud. While trying to get up, he
slipped into the mud again and again.

By the time George was back on the
sidewalk, he was very dirty and very
happy. "Well, I guess I'll just have to go
home for some clean clothes," he chuckled
to himself. "Arithmetic will be over by the
time I get to school!"

The next day, George was one of the first people to arrive at school. His mother, still mad about his muddy adventure, had seen to that.

Soon it was time for the arithmetic game, and George still hadn't thought of a way out of it.

His turn came.

He stared and stared at the card.

"Can you see it all right?" asked Ms. Green. "The problem is, four plus —"

"That's it!" George said. "I can't see the card. I . . . I must need glasses or something."

"Hmmm, maybe you do need your eyes checked. All right, George, sit down. I'll talk to you about this after school. Next — Maria."

When school was over, Ms. Green called George up to her desk. "Is something wrong, George? You don't seem very happy about school these days."

George was silent a moment. "It's that arithmetic game," he said finally. "I hate it."

"Why?"

"It's too hard. I mean, sometimes I know the answers, but I can't say them. It's hard to do it while everyone's watching. I guess I should practice. . . ."

"I think I can help," said Ms. Green. She took the cards from her desk and handed them to George. "Take these home. Ask your parents to help you practice each night. I know you'll get better."

"But what if the other kids find out?"

"It will be our secret. You can keep them for as long as you like. I have another set. Now, George, about your eyes . . ."

"I can see okay," George said. "And
. . . and it wasn't Maria who let the
hamsters out the other day. It was me."

"Maria already told me that. But I was
waiting for you to tell me yourself. I'll see
you tomorrow, George, and don't forget to
practice with those cards."

"That looks like fun," his father said when George showed him the cards. "Let's practice right after dinner."

At first, George had the same trouble. He just couldn't think of the answer, so he took wild guesses.

"Slow down," said his father. "We're in no hurry."

By the next day, George had decided
not to try and avoid arithmetic. When it
was his turn, Ms. Green held up a card
that read "5 + 4."

"Nine?" George squeaked.

Some of his friends turned to look at
him, surprised.

"Right," said Ms. Green.

George kept on standing. On his second
turn, he missed and had to sit down.

That didn't stop George from practicing his arithmetic every night after that. Sometimes his mother helped him, and sometimes his father did. George couldn't believe how much fun arithmetic was getting to be.

One day, George and Maria were the only two players left in the game.
"Come on, George!" someone whispered.
It would be so great if I could win, just this once, George thought to himself.

Ms. Green showed him a card that read "7 + 6."

George looked at the card for a long time, then took a deep breath. "Eleven?"

"I'm sorry," said Ms. Green. "You'll have to sit down."

"Thirteen," Maria called out.

"Very good, Maria," Ms. Green said. "You're the winner, but I think we should give George a cheer too. He's become one of our best players!"

Everyone clapped, and George and Maria beamed.

"You've worked hard," said Ms. Green. "We're glad you're in this class."

"So am I!" George said to himself.

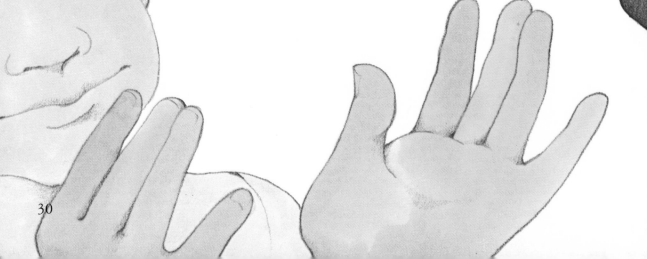